Miss Rafferty's Rainbow Socks

by Annette LeBox

illustrated by Heather Holbrook

HarperCollins*Publishers*Ltd

Produced by Caterpillar Press for
HarperCollins Publishers Ltd
Suite 2900, Hazelton Lanes
55 Avenue Road
Toronto, Canada M5R 3L2

96 97 98 99 First Edition 7 6 5 4 3 2 1

Canadian Cataloguing in Publication Data
LeBox, Annette
Miss Rafferty's rainbow socks
ISBN 0-00-224372-5 (bound)
ISBN 0-00-648148-5 (pbk.)
I. Holbrook, Heather. II. Title.

PS8573.E36M57 1996   jC813'.54   C95-932819-X
PZ7.L43Mi 1996

To my daughter Sara,
my best friend and dancing partner.
Annette LeBox

To my husband Scott,
my source of encouragement and
one-man fan club.
Heather Holbrook

Aldona Rafferty received the rainbow socks on her seventh birthday. An old woman from a nearby village knit them in exchange for some eggs from her chickens. The woman knit the socks in all colors of the rainbow: blue for the sky, rose for the dawn, green for the hills, and yellow for the sun. People said the old woman was poor and used bits and pieces of wool that nobody wanted. But Aldona knew that the woman knitted the socks that way because she liked the happy dance of colors.

Whenever Aldona wore the rainbow socks, she felt like dancing. Her feet felt like wings - she wanted to whirl and dip and sashay and kick up her heels. When Aldona Rafferty grew bigger the socks grew bigger with her. And even when she became an old woman the rainbow socks never wore out. They were as bright and springy as when she first pulled them over her young toes.

Miss Rafferty loved to dance, but she also loved Winnie Latham. The Lathams lived in the farmhouse next door and when Winnie was born, Miss Rafferty pulled on her rainbow socks and went next door to visit.

When Miss Rafferty leaned over Winnie's cradle and hummed a lively dance tune, the baby smiled. When Miss Rafferty held Winnie close and whirled and dipped and sashayed and kicked up her heels, the baby bounced her little legs up and down and laughed.

When Winnie grew older, Miss Rafferty invited the little girl to visit after supper. Sometimes they sipped tea together from pretty china cups. Sometimes Miss Rafferty showed Winnie how to knit with leftover pieces of yarn that nobody wanted. But mostly they danced.

When the sun went down and the moon shone on the roof of the barn, the two friends sat on the porch and sang lively dance tunes. Then Miss Rafferty held out her arms and said, "Shall we?" and Winnie nodded and together they whirled and dipped and sashayed and kicked up their heels.

One summer night when Winnie and Miss Rafferty were wishing on falling stars Winnie said, "I wish for a doll. Martha Milford has nine dolls, but I don't have a single one, not one doll to cuddle and sing to and dance with. Miss Rafferty, how many wishes would it take for a doll?" Miss Rafferty thought for a while.

"I'm not sure, Winnie, let's see." So that night Winnie and Miss Rafferty gazed at the sky and made wishes as the stars tumbled. They caught stardust in their mouths and starshine in their lashes, but after many nights of wishing, Winnie still didn't have a doll.

Winnie showed Miss Rafferty her egg money.

"Miss Rafferty, how many pennies would it take to buy a doll from Harper's General Store?" Miss Rafferty counted the pennies in Winnie's hands. Then she felt the coins in her own pocket. There was not nearly enough. And Miss Rafferty knew that Winnie's family worked hard but they were poor. There was no money for luxuries. No money for dolls.

"Many pennies and a long, long time, Winnie," said Miss Rafferty sadly.

Miss Rafferty thought about Winnie's wishes. She thought about all the dancing her feet had done, all the nights under the moon, whirling and dipping and sashaying and kicking up her heels.

Then Miss Rafferty smiled. She pulled her rainbow socks from her feet, took a pair of scissors from her pocket and with a snip, snip, snip began to unravel the yarn. When she finished, a swirl of rainbow colors lay at her feet. She picked up her knitting needles and began to sing a lively dance tune as her fingers whirled and dipped and sashayed around the yarn. In no time at all, Miss Rafferty knitted the most beautiful rainbow doll in the world. A doll with eyes as blue as the sky, cheeks as rosy as the dawn, a dress as green as the hills, hair as yellow as the sun, and a tiny pair of socks in all the colors of the rainbow.

Miss Rafferty was as happy as a day in spring. She gave the doll to Winnie as a surprise. Winnie held the rainbow doll close and kissed it. Then Winnie whispered, "Shall we?" and in an instant her feet felt like wings.

She whirled and dipped and sashayed and kicked up her heels, and she and the rainbow doll danced the finest dance ever in the sunshiny afternoon.

Sometimes all three of them danced - Miss Rafferty, Winnie and the rainbow doll, whirling and dipping and sashaying and kicking.

When people heard that Miss Rafferty had unraveled her rainbow socks to knit Winnie a doll, they were curious. They wanted to see if the rainbow doll was as wonderful as the rainbow socks. So they made excuses to visit Winnie to catch a glimpse of it.

Martha came to see the rainbow doll, too, and when she saw how pretty it was, she wanted it. She had never owned a rainbow doll and she cried and wheedled and simpered to her father who was the richest man in the village. Finally she stamped her foot and screeched, "I want it!" until her father made a visit to Winnie's father.

Mr. Milford took out ten gold coins from his pocket and lined them up on the table.

"Martha wants your rainbow doll and no other, and I'm bound to please her. The coins are yours if you'll give me the doll."

Winnie's father shook his head.

"The doll is not mine to sell. It belongs to Winnie."

Winnie stood behind the door and listened.

"I won't give you up," she whispered to the rainbow doll. "Not for anything. Especially not to Martha, who has nine dolls already."

Martha's father continued, "I am a rich man. The money means little to me. But for you it would mean enough food for your children for a year and enough firewood to keep you warm for two winters. Surely your family is more important than a doll."

"Nevertheless," said Winnie's father, "the doll is not mine to sell." Then he led Mr. Milford to the door.

"If you change your mind, just come and see me," Martha's father said, putting on his cap.

Winnie told Miss Rafferty about the gold coins. She told her about the bread the coins would put on her mother's table and the fires her father could build on winter nights. She told Miss Rafferty about her father's worried face.

Miss Rafferty and Winnie took the rainbow doll out to the moonlight. Winnie held the doll close and whispered, "Shall we?" and Miss Rafferty nodded, and the two friends and the rainbow doll whirled and dipped and sashayed and kicked up their heels.

But Winnie sang no lively dance tune under the stars. She sang in a voice as sad as the last day of summer.

For a while Martha was happy to have the rainbow doll. She liked to cuddle it and take it to bed with her. She liked to whisper "Shall we?" and feel her legs become as light as wings. She liked to whirl and dip and sashay and kick up her heels as she hummed lively tunes in her head.

But after a time, Martha tired of it. It was only a doll after all, and she had many amusements. Once she left it out in the rain. Another time she threw it at her big brother. Finally, in a temper one evening, she tossed the doll into a ditch where it sunk into thick, dark mud.

When Winnie walked home from school that day, she saw only the yellow yarn of the doll's hair and the pink of a woolen arm from the road. She took the rainbow doll home and washed it with soap and lay it outside to dry in the sun. The colors were a little faded but the doll still looked pretty.

"Oh, I want to keep you, rainbow doll," said Winnie. "But you don't belong to me anymore. Martha's father paid ten gold coins for you." Slowly she walked down the road to Martha's house.

When Martha saw Winnie standing at the door with the rainbow doll, she tossed her head and said, "It's old and ugly. Keep it if you want."
Winnie held the rainbow doll close and whispered, "Shall we?" and she and the rainbow doll danced down the road to Miss Rafferty's farm. Miss Rafferty sat on her porch watching the moon rise.

"Miss Rafferty!" called Winnie. "Rainbow doll's returned! Come and dance."

Miss Rafferty wiggled her toes a little but they felt heavy. She put them back down on the ground and sighed. Winnie stretched out her hand.

"Come, Miss Rafferty, the moon is full. Let's dance together like we used to do!"

But Miss Rafferty just rocked and smiled. "I'm getting old, Winnie. Too old for dancing under the moon. I'll watch you and the rainbow doll dance."
So Winnie and the rainbow doll danced. But Miss Rafferty watching wasn't the same as Miss Rafferty dancing.

Winnie thought about Miss Rafferty's tired feet. She thought about her wonderful rainbow doll. She imagined Miss Rafferty whirling and dipping and sashaying and kicking up her heels.

Then Winnie smiled. She took a pair of scissors from her pocket and with a snip, snip, snip began to unravel the rainbow doll. When she finished, a swirl of rainbow colors lay at her feet. She picked up her knitting needles and began to knit, singing a lively dance tune as her fingers whirled and dipped and sashayed around the yarn. In no time at all, Winnie knitted a new pair of wonderful rainbow socks. She knit them in every color of the rainbow: blue for the sky, rose for the dawn, green for the hills, and yellow for the sun.

Winnie was as happy as a day in spring. She gave the socks to Miss Rafferty.
"Oh, you shouldn't have!" said Miss Rafferty smiling. Then Miss Rafferty stretched out her wrinkly legs and pulled the rainbow socks over her knobby knees. She held out her arms and whispered "Shall we?" and Winnie joined her. And in an instant, Miss Rafferty's stiff legs felt like wings again and the two friends whirled and dipped and sashayed and kicked up their heels until the moon laughed in spite of herself and the milky way sighed a long milky sigh and the stars twinkled in time to the liveliest dance tune ever.